Seely Roland's Collection

Toni Mahoney

AuthorHouse™
1663 Liberty Drive
Bloomington, IN 47403
www.authorhouse.com
Phone: 1-800-839-8640

First published by AuthorHouse 12/1/2010

ISBN: 978-1-4520-9204-1 (sc)

Library of Congress Control Number: 2010916078

Printed in the United States of America

This book is printed on acid-free paper.

authorHOUSE®

Seely Roland loves to explore and discover.

Every day Seely wakes up early in the morning to think about things.

He likes this time of day because the world is very quiet.

Seely listens for the sounds of waking up. He thinks about where he will go and wonders what he will be.

Dressing in the colors of the day, he smiled.

This morning Seely decided he was going to be a collector. He began his search.

He went to the beach and discovered seashells.

Each one had a different pattern and design.

So he began collecting all the seashells.

Then a large loud wave told him, "Seely Roland, you must put them back."

6

Seely did not want to, because he wanted to be a collector.

The wave rolled forward and said, "They can still be your seashells, but they will decorate my beach. You may keep one to remind you of your collection."

So Seely chose
his seashell and
returned the others
to the sand.

Then he placed
his seashell safely
in his pocket and
decided to go
somewhere else to
collect.

That afternoon
walking through
a garden Seely
discovered flowers.

Each one had its own
color and smell.

So he began
collecting all the
flowers.

The warm sun laughed and said, "Seely Roland, you must put them back."

Seely did not want to because he wanted to be a collector.

The sun rose higher and said, "They will still be your flowers, but everyone will smile when they visit my garden. You may keep one to remind you of your collection."

So Seely picked his flower and returned the others to the garden.

He carefully placed his flower in his pocket and decided to go somewhere else to collect.

Late in the day Seely walked into a forest filled with trees.

He discovered that every leaf on every tree was a different size and shape.

So he began collecting all the leaves.

An old tree barked at him, "Seely Roland, you must put them back."

18

Seely did not want to because he wanted to be a
collector.

The old tree slowly bent down and said, "They will still be your leaves, bu[t] we will hold them for you so others may enjoy our shade. You may keep one to remind you of your collection."

20

So Seely decided on a leaf and returned the others to the trees.

He pushed his leaf deep into his pocket and decided to go somewhere else to collect.

That evening Seely was looking up at the sky.

He discovered the stars. Each one was a sparkle of bright light.

So he began to collect all the stars.

The quiet moon whispered, "Seely Roland, you must put them back."

Seely did not want to, because he wanted to be a collector.

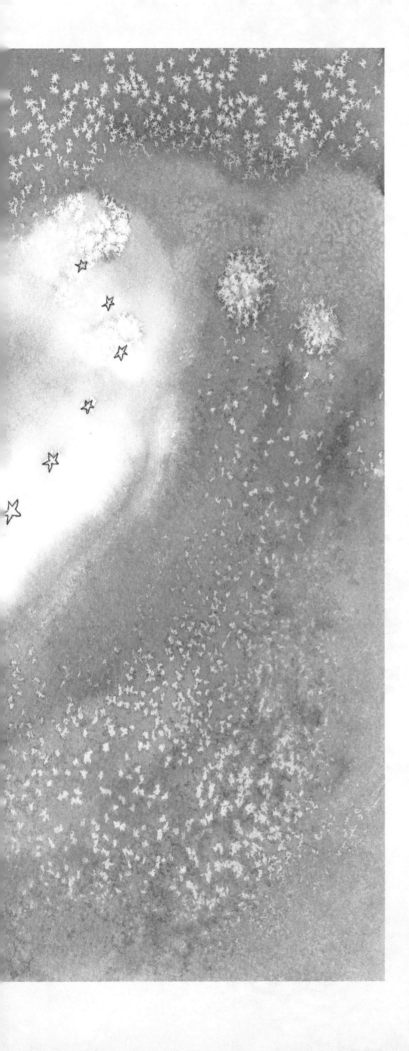

The wise moon told him, "They will still be your stars, but their light will help you to see your collection." Slowly Seely returned every star to the night sky.

Then, using the twinkle of starlight, Seely carefully emptied his pockets.

He looked at his seashell and remembered the beach.

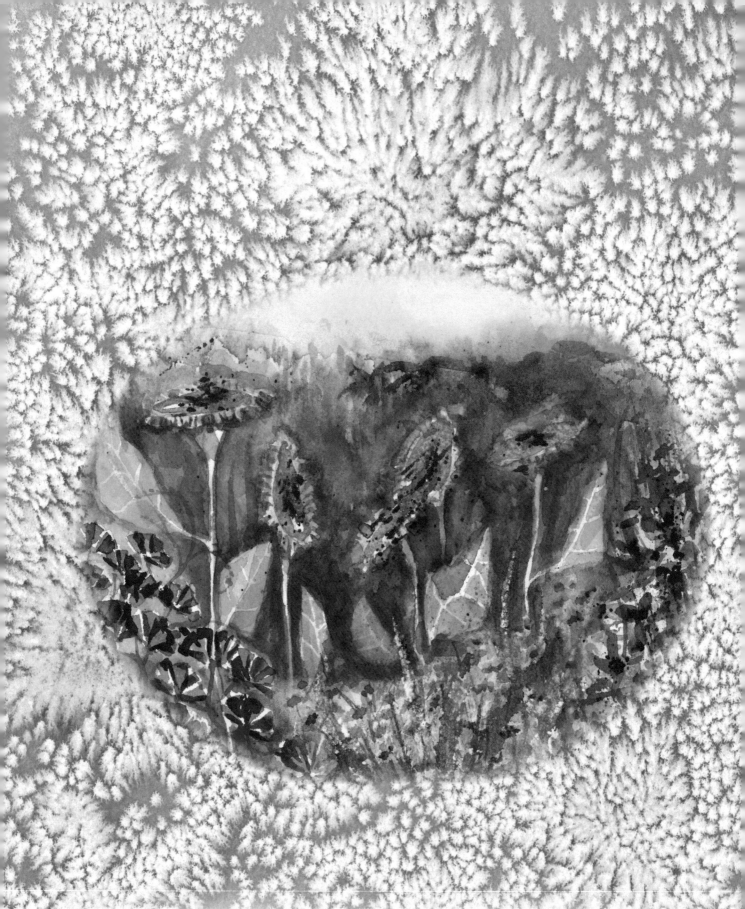

He looked at his flower and remembered the garden.

He looked at his leaf and remembered the forest.

Seely Roland smiled. He had become a great collector.

That night Seely wondered what he would become tomorrow.

This book is dedicated to my family and friends...all of them.

About the Author

Toni Mahoney is an artist from Harrisburg,Pennsylvania. She is inspired by her many siblings,nephews and nieces, years of teaching art to young people, and countless hours and moments of observing and creating art. Seely embodies the spirit of those adventurous collectors of this beautiful life.